Disney's

The Prince

AND THE

Pauper

BY *Teddy Slater*

ILLUSTRATED BY *Phil Wilson*

DISNEP
PRESS

NEW YORK

Printed and bound in the United States of America.
For information address Disney Press,
114 Fifth Avenue, New York, New York 10011.

First Edition

1 3 5 7 9 10 8 6 4 2

Library of Congress Catalog Card Number: 92-56165
ISBN 1-56282-511-9 / 1-56282-512-7 (lib. bdg.)

Disney's

The Prince

AND THE

Pauper

Once upon a time, England was ruled by a wise and good king. The people prospered and were very happy. But by and by, their good king became ill.

His captain of the guards—Captain Pete, as this rogue was called— saw the king's illness as a chance to fatten his own pockets. With the help of his ruthless henchmen, Captain Pete demanded taxes and tribute from the king's poorest subjects. And worst of all, he did it in the king's name.

Among the poorest of the king's subjects was a young peddler named Mickey. From sunrise to sunset he trudged up and down the streets of London, selling scraps of wood for kindling.

Though few Londoners stopped to buy the wood, Mickey never got discouraged. He knew that someday, somehow, things would change. And so they did.

It all began one especially cold winter morning as Mickey, his dog Pluto, and his best friend Goofy stood hungry and shivering in front of the palace....

"Don't feel bad, guys," Mickey said. "One of these days *we'll* be living like kings. We'll have a warm fire and all the turkey, ham, and peas we can eat!"

"Oh yeah!" Goofy chimed in. "And lots of ice cream, cookies, pie, and—"

Goofy stopped in midwish as the royal coach went barreling by, with Captain Pete out front and a noisy bunch of his thugs inside. As the coach bounced along the snowy street, so did a long string of plump sausages hanging out the back.

In a moment the coach disappeared through the palace gates—with Pluto chasing hungrily after it.

"No, Pluto, no!" Mickey cried, just as the gate clanged shut behind his four-footed friend.

KNOCK! KNOCK! Mickey pounded on the gate.

"Who goes there, and whaddaya want?" a voice called from within.

"I just want to get my dog back," Mickey replied.

The gatekeeper peered out at Mickey, gasped in amazement, and quickly opened the gate.

"Y-Y-Your Majesty," the gatekeeper stammered, bowing low to the even more amazed Mickey. "C-c-come in, sire."

Mickey didn't need to be asked twice. He went right in.

The gatekeeper was about to rise again when a scuffed pair of boots appeared in front of his face. The gatekeeper's eyes darted up the scuffed boots and straight into the swarthy face of Captain Pete!

"What do you think this is, open house?" Captain Pete growled.

"But Captain," the gatekeeper said. "That was the prince."

"Oh yeah?" Pete snarled, grabbing the gatekeeper by the scruff of the neck and pointing toward the palace. "Then who's that, numskull?"

The gatekeeper paled as he followed Pete's finger. For there, high up in a lighted window, was someone who looked exactly like Mickey—except for one thing: he was wearing the royal robes!

9

Inside the palace schoolroom the prince was only half-listening to Horace, his boring old tutor. He seemed more interested in watching Donald, the prince's valet, who was puttering around in the corner.

While his tutor droned on (something about Greek—or was it Latin?), the prince pulled out his royal peashooter and fired at Donald.

WHAACK!

Donald squawked as the prince's missile landed on the back of his head.

A moment later a second pea found its mark—WHAACK!—this time on Donald's bottom.

It wasn't until the third pea got him that Donald finally fired back. Unfortunately, his aim was a bit off. Instead of hitting the young prince, he hit the old tutor.

"Now, Donald," Horace scolded.

"The prince started it!" Donald protested. "He—"

"That's enough, Donald!" the tutor broke in, gesturing sternly to the door.

11

As soon as Donald left the room, Horace turned to the prince. "As for you, Your Highness, you know your father is ill and requires rest and quiet," he said. "Now, sire, shall we continue?"

But once again the lesson was interrupted—this time by a ruckus in the palace garden. The prince ran to the window.

Far below, the prince could barely make out Captain Pete scuffling in the snow with a young lad and a dog. "Captain!" he yelled down. "What is the meaning of this uproar?"

"Just some local riffraff, sire," Pete yelled up.

"Even the lowliest subjects of this kingdom deserve respect," the prince chided him. "Unhand that lad and have him brought to me at once!"

Mickey was soon wandering wide-eyed through the palace halls. Shiny suits of armor lined the walls. Crystal chandeliers hung from the ceiling. Everything glimmered and gleamed.

Mickey grinned with delight at the sight of his own reflection in the polished floor. Then he took a quick look around to make sure no one was watching, kicked up his heels, and danced a little jig.

CLANG! Mickey bumped into a suit of armor. The helmet fell off and landed on his head. As he staggered around in the sudden darkness,

Mickey bumped into another suit of armor, which toppled over onto another one, which toppled onto another, which toppled...

Hearing the great hubbub in the hall, the prince dashed out to investigate. "What the devil is going on?" he demanded as another helmet came clanging down onto his own head and over his eyes.

There was a moment of silence while the prince and the pauper groped blindly along the hall.

BANG! The two helmeted heads crashed into each other. The prince and the pauper raised the grilles of their iron hats, then gazed at each other in utter astonishment. There was another short silence, and then in one voice they both screamed: "YOU LOOK JUST LIKE ME!"

"I thought you were…," the prince began.

"I thought you were…," Mickey began.

"Who *are* you?" the prince finally burst out.

16

As soon as Mickey introduced himself, the prince said, "Well, Mickey, I must thank you for saving my life."

"Saving your life?" Mickey echoed.

"I was about to die of boredom when you interrupted my lesson," the prince explained. "Do you know what it's like to be a prince?" he asked. And before Mickey could reply, he told him: "Never a moment to myself. Breakfast at seven. Lessons till lunch. Fencing till tea time...."

Mickey's mouth watered as the prince went on complaining. *Break-fast? Lunch? Tea?* It didn't sound half-bad to the poor, hungry pauper.

But the prince seemed to think Mickey's life sounded even better. "Games all day long. No dreary old lessons," the prince mused wistfully. "Oh, if I could live like you for just one day...."

Suddenly the prince's eyes lit up. "What a grand idea!" he said. "I shall take your place in the streets of London, and you shall be the prince!"

"Th-th-the prince!" Mickey sputtered. "I can't be the prince. I-I wouldn't know how to act."

"Don't worry," the prince assured him. "To govern, you need only to say one of two things: 'That's a splendid idea—I'm glad I thought of it!' and 'Guards, seize him!'"

With no further ado, the prince traded his royal garb for Mickey's pitiful rags and headed for the door. "I'll be back in the wink of an eye!" he promised blithely.

And when Mickey still looked doubtful, the prince held out his hand to reveal the royal ring and said, "You needn't worry. If there's any trouble, all will know me by this."

Mickey gasped at the shimmering gold ring with its royal insignia.

19

But no sooner had the prince pranced through the door than a rough hand reached out and grabbed him.

"Ah, my little pauper," sneered Captain Pete, quite naturally mistaking the prince for Mickey.

"Embarrass me in front of the prince, will ya?" Pete growled, puffing on his big brown cigar and blowing a big black cloud of smoke into the prince's face.

"Pauper!" the prince exclaimed between coughs. "Captain, I am the prince!"

"Oh! Forgive me, Your Highness!" Pete said sarcastically. "Allow me...." And, with a flourish, he picked up the prince and set him down gently — on the seat of a catapult!

"How thoughtful of you, Captain," the prince said, unsuspecting.

"I live to serve!" Pete proclaimed — just before he launched the prince over the castle wall.

PLOP! The prince landed in a fluffy snowbank. Bouncing right up, he dusted himself off and exclaimed, "I'm free! I fooled him! I—"

PLOP! Suddenly the prince found himself back in the snowbank as a warm bundle of fur pounced on his chest and a wet tongue began licking his face. It was Pluto!

But just as suddenly, Pluto realized his mistake. *SNIFF! SNIFF!* This wasn't his master. This was a total stranger! With one more disgusted *SNIFF!* Pluto shambled off.

As soon as the prince was up on his feet again, Goofy ran over. He

turned out to be a lot easier to fool than Pluto.

"Hiya, Mickey," Goofy said.

"Oh, oh yes. That is me. Mickey Mouse," answered the prince.

Although the prince clearly had no idea who Goofy was, Goofy never doubted that the prince was his old friend. Even when the prince came right out and asked, "Could I have your name?" Goofy figured he was kidding and replied, "Har! Har! What's the matter with the one ya got?"

Then, before Goofy could ask any more difficult questions, the prince bid him a quick good-bye and hurried away down the street.

At that very moment the real Mickey was trying to concentrate on the prince's geography lesson. But his mind kept wandering to another subject—food!

Just as Horace asked, "In what country is the city of Istanbul?" Donald entered the room carrying a large silver platter.

"Istanbul is…it's uh, well, it's in…" Mickey's voice trailed off as Donald began carving the plump, juicy bird on the plate. A mouth-watering aroma wafted across the room, and Mickey burst out, "Turkey!"

"Turkey is correct!" Horace said approvingly as Mickey made a mad dash for his long-awaited dinner.

Meanwhile, the prince was learning a lesson of his own—that life outside the palace wasn't just fun and games. For one thing, not all dogs were as mild mannered as Pluto. When he tried playing fetch with a mangy mutt's bone, the prince found himself pursued by a whole pack of angry hounds. He finally escaped by jumping over a fence…

…only to find himself in the middle of an unusual tug-of-war. A poor woman was desperately trying to stop two of Pete's guards from stealing her last chicken.

"Halt!" the prince cried. "I am your prince, and I command you to unhand that hen."

The guards took one look at the pauper and laughed uproariously. "Oh, Your Highness," one of them said mockingly, "I think ya forgot yer crown!" And with that, he smashed an overripe pumpkin onto the prince's head and ran off with the chicken.

A small child approached and helped the stunned prince to his feet.

"I can't believe it," said the prince. "Stealing in the king's name!"

The prince was still standing there when a big open wagon filled with food came clattering down the street. "Make way for the royal provisioner!" the driver shouted. "Come on, move it!"

But even as the townspeople scattered, the prince jumped right into the path of the oncoming horse. "Halt! I am the prince!" he cried again— only this time he held up his royal ring. "I command you to surrender your entire inventory." The driver gasped, and the crowd slowly knelt down and bowed to the prince. Then the driver backed away as the prince climbed aboard the wagon and began tossing food to the hungry peasants.

Minutes later, Pete's guards returned. "You there!" the head guard pointed to the prince. "You're under—" *SMACK!* A piece of watermelon hit the guard in the face before he could arrest the prince.

And while one peasant threw another melon at the guard, the prince swung a huge leg of lamb at another. Hams, rutabagas, chickens, and

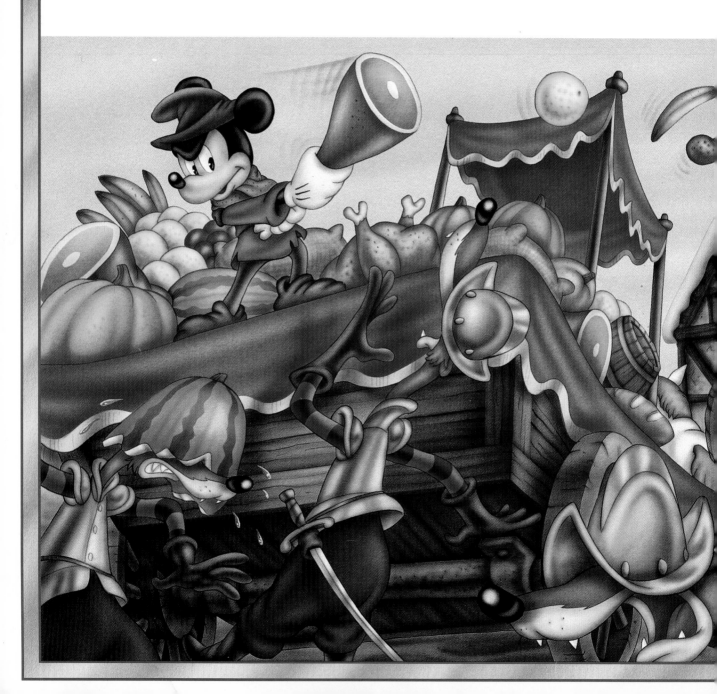

chops flew through the air as the other peasants joined in the battle. But their makeshift weapons were no match for the guards' steel swords.

Goofy appeared at the edge of the crowd just as the guards were about to close in on the prince. "Hang on, Mick," Goofy hollered. "I'm coming!" And with that, he leapt onto a barrel and began to run—and roll! He rolled right into the pack of guards who had surrounded the prince.

As the guards screamed and scattered, Goofy snatched up the prince and began to roll backward. He rolled over the guards and kept on rolling until—CRASH!—he rolled right into the provisioner's cart! The frightened horse reared up suddenly and took off down the street with Goofy and the prince hanging on to the cart for dear life.

The guards hurried back to Captain Pete's quarters to give him the bad news.

"All I know is he acted like a nobleman and he had the royal ring," the head guard said.

"So it *was* the prince I booted out," Pete said uneasily.

"You threw the prince out?" The guard shrieked with laughter and chanted, "You're in trouble! You're gonna get it!"

Pete reached over and grabbed the guard by the throat, pulling him close. Then an evil grin flashed across Pete's face. "Not if he doesn't come back alive!" he chortled.

Back at the palace, Mickey was just receiving some bad news of his own. "Your Highness," Horace said, "your father is in his last hours and wishes to see you at once."

"Oh, we'd better tell the prince," Mickey replied without thinking. "He'd want to see him."

Horace gave Mickey a strange look. "You *are* the prince, sire," he pointed out.

I'll explain everything! Mickey thought as he followed Horace down the hall and into the king's somber bedchamber. *The king will understand.*

But it wasn't that easy.

"My son," a soft voice called before Mickey could utter a word.
"Come closer." Mickey hesitated but moved slowly toward the king's
bed in the dim light. "From the day you were born I have tried to pre-
pare you for this moment. I shall be gone soon, and you will be king. You
must promise me that you will rule the land from your heart—justly and
wisely."

Deeply moved by the passionate plea, Mickey took the king's out-
stretched hand in his and said, "I promise."

Head bowed, Mickey walked quietly out of the king's room. With a heavy heart, he moved toward a large window in the corridor and stared out at the twinkling lights of London. "I've got to find the prince," he said to himself—or so he thought.

"Good day, my phony prince," Pete jeered, grabbing Mickey's shoulder and spinning him all the way around.

"Unhand me!" Mickey ordered in his most princely manner.

But Pete only held him tighter. "Shaddup!" the cruel captain said. "Now that our dearly departed king is out of my way, you're going to do

every little thing I say. 'Cause if you don't…"

Captain Pete didn't even bother to finish his threat. He didn't have to. He simply picked Mickey up and pointed toward a dark corner, where a yelping bundle of fur was tied up with heavy rope.

"Pluto!" Mickey cried.

"Get the picture?" said Pete with a menacing smile.

For once, Mickey was speechless.

The silence was finally broken by the sound of church bells tolling the king's death.

From Goofy's hovel on London Bridge, the prince also heard the mournful song. Opening a window, he called out to a boatman down below. "You, sir, what's happened?"

"The king is dead, and the prince is to be crowned at once," the man reported.

"Father," the prince whispered sadly, turning from the window. Slowly he walked back to the fireplace and sat down, wiping a tear from his eye.

"Now it's up to me to right the wrongs I've seen—children going hungry, corruption everywhere." He pulled the royal ring from his pocket and slipped it on with determination.

Then and only then did Goofy realize that the guest in his home wasn't Mickey. "Gawrsh, you really are the prince," he gulped. "Sire, your wish is my command."

"Come, now," the prince continued. "We must return to the palace at once."

But before the two were out the door, Captain Pete and his guards burst in.

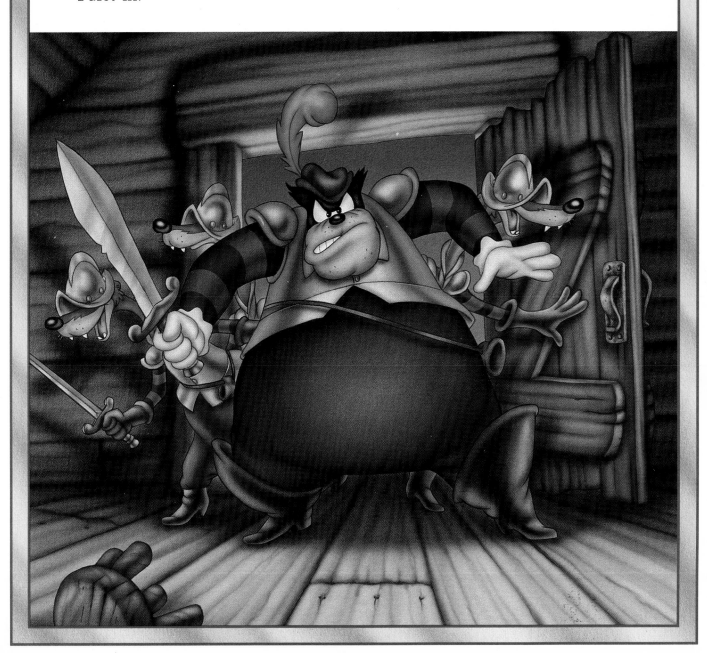

Goofy did his best to defend the prince, but this time it wasn't enough. While half the guards sent Goofy flying out the window, the other half surrounded the prince and forced him out the door.

"To the dungeon," Captain Pete yelled to his guards. Then he turned to the prince. "And after the pauper is crowned, it will be adieu to you!"

The guards threw the prince into the palace dungeon, where Donald had already been imprisoned.

"Your Highness, Your Highness, we're saved!" Donald cried, throwing his arms around the prince.

Suddenly the door to the dungeon clanged shut.

"Wait a minute, you're in here, too," Donald said. "Your Highness, we're doomed!"

"Listen!" said the prince. They could hear the sound of trumpets playing a fanfare. "The coronation!"

A new king—but not the true king!—was about to be crowned.

"I demand that you open this door immediately," the prince yelled to the guard outside the cell.

Suddenly and silently a dark shadow slid across the wall—the executioner's shadow!

"Looks like the boss ain't wasting any time," the guard snickered. He waved the black-robed figure toward the dungeon door.

The executioner took a step forward, and then another. And then he stepped right into a bucket and tripped! The ax flew out of his hand and landed just inches above the guard's head.

"Ahyuck—sorry," came the voice beneath the hood.

As the executioner pried the ax out of the wall, the handle came down on the guard's head with a *THWACK!*

The minute the stunned guard slumped to the floor, the executioner reached up a gloved hand and tore off his hood.

The prince took one look at the smiling face beneath the mask and gasped, "Goofy!"

"Gawrsh," Goofy greeted the prince. "Just sit tight, li'l buddy," he said, pulling out a giant key ring from the pocket of his robe. "I'll have ya outta there in a jiffy."

But back in the coronation hall, time was running out for Mickey. Unless he did something soon, the little pauper would be crowned king and Captain Pete would continue to pillage the kingdom and its people.

The archbishop was about to place the crown on the pauper's head when Mickey looked up and saw Captain Pete's face in the crowd.

"*STOP!*" Mickey shouted. His cry echoed throughout the cavernous room.

The archbishop stopped.

"Look, I'm the prince, right?" said Mickey, hopping down from the throne. "And whatever I order must be done, right?"

"Yes, sire," the archbishop agreed.

"Well, then," said Mickey, pointing to Pete, "the captain is an insolent scoundrel! Guards, seize him!"

"Seize *him*!" said Pete, pointing to Mickey. "He's an impostor."

43

But before the guards could seize anyone, a regal voice declared, "But *I'm* not, Captain!"

All eyes turned to a high window ledge at the back of the room, where the real prince now stood. Suddenly the prince leapt from his perch, grabbed hold of the chandelier, and went flying down to the ground right in front of Pete.

"W-w-wait a minute, Your Majesty," said Pete. "I can explain everything."

"Very well, go ahead," said the prince.

But as the prince awaited the explanation, Pete leaned down and snatched up the carpet beneath his feet. Once again, the prince went flying.

But now someone else swung gallantly from the chandelier overhead. "Geronimo!" Goofy cried as he and Donald rushed to the prince's aid. Even Pluto joined in the fray when a guard's misfired arrow sliced through his leash.

Swords slashed, teeth gnashed, and fists flew as Mickey and his gang struggled to overcome Pete and his guards. But Pete finally cornered the prince and was raising his sword for the final blow when suddenly Pluto's teeth clamped on to the seat of his pants! The crowd roared with laughter as Pete's pants fell around his ankles, and it was only a matter of seconds before the prince disarmed the evil captain.

The room was silent for a minute, and then: "Boy, am I glad to see you!" the two look-alikes chorused.

The archbishop's eyes darted from Mickey to the prince and back again. "B-but, you see…," he began. "I…I…Which?… G-good heavens. Which one is which?"

But Pluto had no trouble telling them apart. With a welcoming "*WOOF!*" he bounded over to his master.

"I guess there's no fooling you, boy," Mickey said, scooping Pluto up in his arms.

Only then did the archbishop finally place the crown on the rightful heir's head.

"The king is crowned!" his subjects cheered. "Long live the king!"

And so he did. With his loyal companions Mickey and Goofy at his side, the new king ruled his country just as his father had…justly and wisely.